Dark Hearts - Dark Hearts

Dark Hearts
Dark Hearts

By Helen Glenister

A Mightier Than the Sword UK Publication

Paperback Edition

ISBN Kindle 978-1-7385919-1-6
ISBN Paperback 978-1-99-117196-2

Cover Design by Get Covers

Dark Hearts - Dark Hearts

Introduction

When people tell you that they're afraid of the dark, it's not the night they are really afraid of. It's what is lurking out in the darkness that they fear. Fear of what cannot be seen or even understood for the most part. But the truth is that though we try and explain away our fear of monsters, of creatures that skirt the boundaries of natural and supernatural, we are scared for a reason.

That ancient fear of being hunted is even harder for modern man to reconcile with; after all, man is master of all he surveys. He has replaced God with Mammon, he thrives on entitlement and satisfying his own selfish needs regardless of how it affects anyone else; how could there possibly be anything out there that he doesn't know about, can't explain away, or that anything could possibly be hunting him?

Dark Hearts - Dark Hearts

<u>PROLOGUE</u>

Lucian Dark stood out on the balcony under the cold watchful light the of moon. He watched the bustling streets below, waiting for something. He wasn't sure what it was that had drawn him out on this night, but he knew that whatever it was, it was not something he could afford to miss.

It had been a long time since he had felt called by anything. His life had not been easy when he had been alive, and arguably it had become more challenging since he was turned. He had very few memories of his life before he was a vampire, but those he did have were memories that he could not escape.

He remembered his father, a kind man that had been killed by a feral and left Lucian homeless, a man stealing to survive who became adept at talking his way into lady's beds, and robbing them before the morning came. He remembered the beatings he had taken at the hands of brutal men, the warmth of the touch of a woman's skin and her pleasure moans in the depths of night. But none of these things meant much to him now.

His memories now were of his life as an immortal lord, the son of one of the great vampires, and the history of their clan was the only history or heritage that he cared for. But in all that his vampiric father had imparted to him, the story of two lovers was the one that he prized above all else.

CHAPTER 1

"My boy, sit down, for I am about to tell you the greatest love story ever told," his father said as he grabbed Lucian by the arm and half-led, half-dragged the boy to sit by the stove. The small hut was not much of a home, but it was enough to keep out the worst of the foul winter weather.

Lucien was more than a boy, he was fifteen years old and in a few weeks would be starting life as journeyman blacksmith, but to his father, Lucien Dark would always be a boy. His father had worked hard to raise his son after his wife had died giving birth to him. It had been a tough road for his father to walk, but it was certainly one he had been happy to.

He was a chimney sweep and for his early years. Lucien had worked with his father, climbing up inside the chimneys and cleaning the hard to reach places, but as he got older and the risk of him getting stuck inside the chimneys became greater, his father had apprenticed him to the local blacksmith.

Neither professions seemed to fit the demeanour of the young man, but life was hard for those without money or education, and so he had resigned himself to his lot in life. He imagined that he would one day marry the blacksmith's daughter and the pair of them would have a passable life together. The idea of the match had pleased his father, and so he had taken to sitting his son down and telling him stories of love, tragedy and loss. One of the stories had been the story of how he had met his mother, but some of them seemed to be more like legends than true to life events.

"Is this story one that you have made up?" Lucien asked him a heavy sigh as he settled down on a wooden stool close to the fire.

"I don't have a mind for making up stories, boy, I only tell you tales other people have told me. I can't make them up, but I can remember them. You'd do well to remember them to and see how telling them brings you more friends, especially down the pub," his father chided him.

"Now, keep your mouth shut whilst I tell you this tale. It began with a boy. His name was Durant, and was born centuries before us. His mother died, much like yours, bringing her son into the world. He wasn't a remarkable boy but the sacrifice of his mother made him even more precious in the eyes of his father. His father was not a rich man, and he had lived a hard life before Durant had come into the world. By the time Durant was five, it was clear that his father would not live to see his sixth birthday.

Losing his parents so early in life would have seemed unfair, if the boy had been old enough to understand what it meant. But in his world he was simply left alone with no one to feed him or tuck him in at night. To begin with, the people of the town helped to take care of the boy, but as he grew up, he showed no inclination of learning a trade or doing anything of value. So the people turned their back on Durant and it was not long before he lost his home and he found himself exiled from the town he had grown up in.

He took to stealing from travellers and moved from village to town, for many years, until he became a man. As a man he was a more attractive than those who worked hard in fields or over forges. He had searing blue eyes and blonde hair that shone in the sun when he had the inclination to wash the grim from it.

Whenever he arrived in a new place, women would turn their heads and giggle as he passed. Walking place to place kept him fit and strong, without an ounce of fat on his frame. So it wasn't long before he found himself being offered money to pleasure women for a single night. If his father had lived to see his son become a prostitute, it would have killed him, but Durant saw no shame in sleeping with women if they could afford to pay for his company.

He was nearly twenty years old by the time he came to the walls of one of the smaller cities. He had always avoided cities as a child as they were patrolled by watchmen and guards of the noble that ruled there, but as a man, he knew that there were far more women for him to seduce and earn a living from in the city than in the towns and villages that were scattered about the countryside.

He forged a reputation for himself that earned him many older, wealthy clients, and with that reputation came risks. He soon found himself being chased out of houses by sons worried about their inheritance, or young hopefuls that wanted to wed the widows that could take care of them.

He had altercations in the streets and threats, but nothing too serious happened until one of the darker nights of winter. Durant had been visiting the home of a rich widow, she was a young woman who was not interested in marriage, but wanted a son. It had not been long since her husband had died and she felt that sleeping with Durant could provide her with the child she wanted and people would believe that it was the child of her departed husband.

They had both been careful to keep their assignations quiet, but there had been a few instances where men that had their eyes on the young woman's fortune had warned Durant to stay away from the house.

He would arrive at the house during the dead of night and leave long before morning, but as he left the house on this black night, he heard footsteps following behind him. He walked faster, trying to reach the room he had taken not far from the district, but as he sped up, so did the footsteps behind him, and they were getting closer.

He could feel fear rising in his chest, blood pounding in his ears and he was close to panicking.

Durant was about to break into a run when the footsteps stopped. He paused to look around, turned to look back and saw the street was clear. He breathed a sigh of relief, but as he went to continue on his way, he found himself face-to-face with what could only be described as a rabid monster.

It had red piercing eyes, long claws and teeth that were sharp enough to pierce metal. Durant tried to flee, but the claws sank deep into his arms and back and dragged him from the street into the dank surroundings of an unlit alleyway.

Durant tried to scream and call for help, but the monster bit into his neck and ripped at his vocal chords. He was certain that he was destined to die, when a sharp whistle shattered through his mind and the monster ceased its attack. The whistle came again and then all of a sudden the monster vanished.

Durant lay in the alley, losing blood, and wished he had done more with his short life. He was so close to death that he did not hear the approach of a woman. She sauntered into the alley almost silently. Her thick cape swishing about her body was she moved. Her feet moved lightly over the cobbles as though she were not even touching them at all.

Her scent was sweetly perfumed, and her voice was soft as she knelt beside Durant and whispered in his ear.

"I can save you from death if you wish. All I ask is that you pledge yourself to me for all eternity."

Durant wasn't sure if what she was saying was real or a temptation from the devil, but he did not care. He nodded his head and felt her lips on his neck before he passed out.

<u>Chapter 2</u>

When Durant opened his eyes, he found himself in a four-poster bed, the furnishings about him were rich and lavish. A fire burned in the grate of a grand fireplace, but he felt neither warm nor cold.

His hand went to his throat and found that it had completely healed. So had the damage to his back and arms.

"Do not worry, you are quite whole again," the voice of the woman he had heard from the alley spoke from the shadows of the doorway.

"Who are you?" Durant asked groggily as he tried to sit up. He found he could not move as his wrists and ankles were all tied, one to each of the bed posts.

"I am simply known as the countess by those outside of these walls. But you may call me Daciana - or mistress," the voice replied and Durant felt one of her fingers stroking his cheek.

"Where am I? What happened to me?" Durant asked as he tried to pull his head away from her hand.

"You are in my castle. You have lived in the shadow of it for your entire life, but now you are one of my sired ones, it shall be your home. As to what happened to you. That is a longer story than you might think. You were attacked in the street by one of my sired ones turned feral. He was always somewhat unpredictable but after he had gorged himself on blood, he lost the very slender grasp on the control of the demon within and simply went mad with bloodlust. I had to put the creature down as there was no regaining his sanity when he lost it in such a manner. You were one of his victims that I offered to save in return for your pledge of being mine for eternity," the countess replied.

"You saved me? But then why do I feel nothing

and why am I tied to this bed?" Durant demanded. He truly did feel different and when the countess had spoken of the demon within, he realised that he understood what she meant. There was a hunger that was growing inside of him, a beast that seemed possessed of it's own wants and desires that he had to control lest it overwhelm him.

"I gave you eternal life, or rather I should say unlife. You are not truly alive any longer. Your heart does not beat as it did before, it is slow, slower than you may ever have felt before, and you can no longer create your own blood. Instead, you must feed on the blood of the living to replenish and sustain you. You can go months without feeding, and even decades if necessary. You will become weaker and may even fall into a hundred year slumber if you starve yourself, but you will not die if you refuse to feast. The hunger may drive you mad, but you will not die from it," the countess explained.

"Then I will never have to eat or drink again, except for blood?" Durant asked.

"That is correct. You can eat and drink whatever you wish but there is little point as your body gains nothing from the sustenance. You are almost invulnerable, except for sunlight, sanctified items, water and ground, and a wooden stake to your heart. Those are the only items that can kill you. You will find that your desires have also changed somewhat. You will have new ambitions to go with your new life, some will revolve around pain, others will revolve around slaking your sexual desire, then there are ambitions that are all about gaining power - whether that is power over your own kind or dominion over the human cattle upon which we feast, who can say. But your life here will be quite different from the life you led before. You are stronger, faster, and have abilities that humans can only dream of," the countess said.

"Then I am tied to this bed as part of your games

of power?" Durant asked, feeling himself engorge at the thought of the woman wielding her power over him in bed.

"Hardly. You are tied up as when a new blood is first sired, there is always a chance that they might turn feral. Not every human that has been born into our world has been able to regain their mind or even survive the process. Those that cannot regain their mind during their conversion are feral children that must be destroyed. Tying you down would have made it much easier for me to destroy you, had you proven to be a mistake," the countess laughed. "It would have been a waste, but as you survived, I suppose that it could be one of the ways in which you can show me your undying devotion - since it excites you so."

For the first time since he opened his eyes the countess stepped into his field of vision. She was a tall woman with high cheekbones. She did not look young, but she did look hauntingly beautiful. Her dark hair curled about her face, her eyes were a mixture of blue and green that caused them to look enchanted. Her skin was flawless and almost translucent.

Her body was slender and firm, but there was a muscle tone to her that betrayed the strength of her vampiric body.

Her lips were the most alluring part of her body, crimson and full, they cried out to Durant. He wanted to feel them caressing his skin, pressing hard against his own lips, and most of all, he wanted to feel his hardened cock slipping between those lips as she took him deep into her throat.

Her lips twisted into a cruel smile, as though she were reading the lustful thoughts in his mind.

"You should also know that in not producing blood, without feeding, you will be unable to stiffen," she said grabbing hold of his half-erect member with her long and slender fingers. The firmness of her grasp caused him to shudder with delight.

"How do I feed?" Durant gasped.

"I shall teach you that in time. There is no hurry for you to learn everything in one night. For now, drink from this goblet. It is blood taken from the cut throats of two virgins that were given to me as scullery maids. Neither girl was willing to work so their blood shall sustain you, until I have decided whether you are worth keeping or not," the countess said as her fingers released his penis. She picked up a large, gold goblet from the table that stood beside the bed and grabbed hold of Durant's hair, forcing his head up to drink from the goblet she pressed to his lips.

The scent of sweet and fresh blood filled his nostrils and he felt the hungry beast in the depth of his spirit growl and writhe with delight.

He greedily drank the contents of the goblet and felt an explosion of power release inside of him. It was like nothing he had ever felt before in his life and the feeling of it threatened to overwhelm everyone of his senses. He growled and grunted with an animalistic savagery that caused him to thrash against the bonds that held him to the bed.

The countess watched him with great interest. The internal battle being waged between the civilised mind and the vampire beast was one that she had witnessed many times and this man before her was the most promising creature she had ever sired. He was strong and experienced in pleasuring women, but more than that, he promised to be the perfect hunter who could bring fresh humans into her house, new thralls and most importantly, young women.

The countess began to undress as she watched him, the unleashed rage of the newly sired tasting fresh blood was always the most erotic experience with any of her sired ones. Her pussy was wet with anticipation as her clothes all fell to the floor and she advanced upon the writhing body of Durant.

He was already undressed. His clothes had been

all but destroyed during the attack in the village, and there was no need for him to be clothed. He did not need them for warmth and Daciana wanted to see the effect that her presence, words and the blood had on his body.

She reached out and slowly ran her hand down his bare chest, her fingertips brushing gently over his skin.

As Durant felt her hands on his body, his mind came into sharp focus, the desire of the beast to feed had been replaced by the desire to fuck.

He felt her hand take hold of his cock, her fingers wrapping around the shaft and for a long, lingering moment, she slowly brought her mouth down so that her lips rested against the tip.

"Oh God, please," Durant begged and then gasped with pleasure as he felt her lips slowly parting and his rapidly engorging member being allowed into her mouth.

He felt her sucking on his cock, her hand squeezing firmly at the base whilst her lips and tongue moved up and down his quivering member.

The pleasure of being in her mouth was far more intense than he ever remembered the act being when he was alive, and when she stopped and released his cock without ceremony and almost threw it aside, he cried out angrily.

"Patience, child," the countess said as she mounted Durant. He felt her hands grabbing hold of his member again, the now fully erect cock only needed guiding to the wet opening of her pussy.

She slowly lowered herself onto his throbbing dick, pushing him deep into her body, a satisfied groan escaping her lips.

Durant grabbed at the sheets on the bed and bit his lip,trying not to cum the instant he was inside of her. He felt like he had never had sex before, as none of his experience had prepared him for the countess.

She watched his reactions with great satisfaction, pausing to ensure that everything she did was being appreciated.

Then she began to ride him. Her body moving with a practised rhythm, using the angle of her body to not only pleasure herself but Durant as well. She squeezed his cock inside of her, so that every thrust gave a new wave of ecstasy to them both. Durant did his best not to climax for as long as he could, but there was only so much that he could do to stave off the inevitable.

The countess did not stop when Durant came inside of her. She kept riding him until she brought herself to climax. Durant had expected to disappoint her when he exploded deep in her pussy, but he did not become soft after he came. He remained hard until the countess screamed as she orgasmed.

Had he the capacity to think at all during their encounter, he would have thought it odd that his body had not reacted the way that he expected, but as the countess collapsed beside him on the bed, he was only glad that she had been satisfied in their first time together.

He did feel tired, but he closed his eyes and when he opened them again, he was alone in the darkness and the bonds tying him to the bed were gone.

CHAPTER 3

There was a great deal that Durant had to learn about his new body and life, and the majority of his early education was focused on sex. The countess would bring him fresh blood to drink in a goblet and then fuck him until she was satisfied.

Durant became better at lasting longer until he was able to hold off his explosive release until he was making the countess climax. The orgasms did not come more quickly, but the pleasure became more intense each time.

After months of nothing but days and nights of sex with his vampire mistress, the countess began to unveil some of the secrets of their powers and just why the sex was so much better as a vampire than it had been as a mere human.

"We have the power to enthral, quite literally to take control of the minds of others. We can make others see things that seem to be real, feel things more intensely, or simply dominate and control them completely. When I decide I want you to fuck me, I simply reach inside of your mind and augment the pleasure you are feeling. The more pleasure you feel, the harder you try to satisfy me. The harder you try to satisfy me, the more I enhance your pleasure. We shall find you some toy to play with so that you may practice your own abilities. But before that, I shall teach you to feed," the countess had explained.

"Please, teach me all that you know mistress," Durant begged.

"Very well, come we shall go out this evening and find some suitable prey for you," the countess said with satisfaction.

Durant spent the whole day impatiently waiting for night to fall so that they could step out of the castle.

He had no way of knowing how much time had passed since he had first been turned, but the countess was not risking taking him back to the village he had grown up in.

Instead, she ordered her carriage to be brought and they drove to a village that was over an hour away from the castle.

The streets were full of people as the carriage rolled down the main road of the village. Some form of festival was being celebrated and there was a great deal of laughter and excitement in the air.

The countess smiled as she saw all of the people celebrating with great abandon. It was not a warm smile, but one that was cruel and calculated.

"Come, we shall walk amongst the rabble, find something that peaks your interest and I shall do the rest. You will feel the desire to feed as you pass the prey, but you must control it. If you cannot, then you are of no use to me and are no better than a feral," the countess warned.

Durant nodded meekly, feeling that he could

easily follow the instructions of his mistress. The moment that the carriage door opened and Durant stepped out of the confines to the street below, he felt the beast in the pit of his stomach awaken.

It was not a gentle awakening from slumber, but an explosion of need and greed that made him feel dizzy and as though he was not fully in control of himself. He grabbed hold of the door and felt the wood splintering under the pressure of his fingers.

"Control yourself," the countess warned as she pushed him aside and alighted from the carriage.

She seemed to be unaffected by the proximity of so much prey and the need to feed seemed to not exist in her.

Durant wondered how long it had taken for her to master her abilities and how old she truly was. But now was not the time for such a question.

He tried to focus on his mistress and following her in an effort to control his hunger. After half an hour of walking amongst the humans, Durant began to feel more able to control himself and he began to take stock of those around him.

There were few women there that were of the right age to appeal to him. Most were either too old or too young. But after an hour, there were two girls that he found suitably attractive and seemed to be poor enough to be in need of work at the countess' castle.

Durant pointed out the two girls and the countess had soon recruited them to her service, along with three young men that seemed to be of a similar look and build to Durant.

He did not comment, but he felt a little hurt that she seemed to be already trying to replace him.

"Choose one of the two girls to bring back tonight," the countess hissed in his ear. "It is up to you to convince her to accompany you."

Durant nodded and steeled his nerve. There was no discernible difference between the two girls. They were both mildly attractive, of a equal weight, and neither of them held much of a spark, but their blood called to him.

He tried to quiet his mind and found that it almost did not matter which of the two girls he picked, so he approached the girl that was closer.

"Young master, your mother has asked us to come tomorrow, is there something the matter?" the girl asked nervously as Durant approached her.

"There is nothing wrong," Durant assured her in what he hoped was a soothing voice. She seemed to relax slightly at his words, and he bowed slightly to her. "I was hoping that you might wish to accompany to the castle tonight, so that I may become better acquainted with you."

His voice was genteel and the offer seemed to delight the young woman, so much so that she stifled a squeal of delight.

"I must go home at once and fetch my things,"

she said. But Durant offered her his arm.

"We shall send for your things in the morning. Come, we shall be departing soon," he smiled at her, and the girl smiled back, eagerly taking his arm.

There was no cry of alarm and no objection as Durant escorted the girl to the carriage and helped her inside.

The countess was already inside with two of the young men she had recruited. Once Durant and the girl were inside the carriage, the door was closed and it lurched away from the village, heading to the castle.

As they arrived at the castle, the two men were sent to report to the butler for their duties. Durant had never thought about the servants at the castle, but it was clear that there were people working there, prey that the countess had kept hidden from him.

With the two men sent away, the countess instructed the girl to follow her and Durant fell into step behind them.

She led them both to a small sitting room on one side of the house that seemed to be rarely used and shut the door behind them.

There was a fire lit in the room, and candles were also burning, providing a low light that seemed to be perfect for what was about to happen.

The countess invited the girl to sit beside Durant on the sofa and then turned to Durant.

"Look into her eyes and then look past them, feel her desires and then seize upon the one you wish to control," the countess whispered in Durant's ear.

He felt a rush of desire as Daciana's lips brushed against his ear. He turned to the girl, who looked confused at the situation that she now found herself in.

Durant looked into her eyes and felt her fear beginning to rise, but he looked past that and found the spark of lust that had caused her to follow him so readily. He reached out with his mind and took hold of that part of her.

"Good, now seduce her," the countess instructed and stepped back so that she might watch Durant.

"Please, sir," the girl protested weakly, but her breath was catching in her chest. Her hands were trembling and she was not pulling away from him.

"You are so beautiful," Durant whispered to her as her slowly reached his hand out to stroke the inside of her thigh. "I have never met a woman who can compare to your beauty. You have captivated my heart and will leave me a broken man if I cannot have you."

The girl blushed and leant towards Durant. Her breathing was more laboured and Durant could smell the sweet scent of her wet pussy, even through the layers of clothing she wore.

He gently took her chin in his hand and kissed her, a fleeting brush of his lips against hers, and he then moved his lips to her cheek and then slowly down her neck, causing the girl to gasp.

"Good, now follow your instincts, but do not let

go of her mind. Enhance her pleasure as you feed," the countess instructed with pride.

Durant reached a point on the girl's neck that seemed to scream out to him and he paused. His fangs hovered over her throat before he plunged them deep into the flesh of her neck.

She cried out in surprise, but Durant did not release her mind, he held on to the the spark of lust and felt it growing stronger in his mind's grasp.

The girl moaned as he drank her blood, the desire to feed was so strong that he did not know how much he was consuming or when to stop, but he trusted the countess would know. the girl's moaning grew loader with each passing moment until the countess placed her hand on his shoulder.

"Enough. Now look at her. You have made her dizzy from the loss of her blood, you have heightened her pleasure to such a degree, now fuck her. She will feel pleasure like she will never know again and she will be your willing slave," the countess said with satisfaction and watched as Durant fumbled to undress the girl and himself.

He then paused as he looked at the naked girl that lay on the floor.

"What are you waiting for?" the countess asked.

"For her to beg, I cannot fuck her if she resists me," Durant said.

"Then ask her what she wants," the countess said with mild annoyance.

Durant leaned over her body, his hard cock pressing against her wet pussy, desperate to be inside of her.

"Tell me what you want," Durant whispered to the girl.

"I want you inside me," the girl moaned, and it was all that Durant needed.

Daciana watched the pair as Durant fucked the young girl. She felt no jealousy, he belonged to her and he would be hers for eternity. Letting him feed and enthral virgins was a necessary part of their life.

After a few minutes of listening to the girl scream and moan, the countess left the pair to their fun and went in search of her two new toys.

CHAPTER 4

Durant's life began to fall into a routine of sex with his mistress and sex with his thralls. He was only ever allowed two thralls at a time, though he did not know how many Daciana had, but he suspected she had far more than he could imagine.

As the thralls aged, they began to lose their appeal and the countess showed Durant how to dispose of them when they had lived past their usefulness.

But this life of sex and feeding began to feel somewhat hollow and pointless. Durant began to question his immortality and the point of it all.

100 years had passed since he had first been turned and no others had been sired to his knowledge since the countess had sired him.

It had taken a century for Durant to become bored with being the cloistered toy of Daciana. She seemed to have so much to do with her time, far more than the sex and feeding that Durant was allowed to fill his days.

Daciana seemed to be less interested in him than she had been in the beginning as well, so she spent less time watching him or even speaking to him. Once her desires had been satisfied, she seemed not to care what Durant did.

He was also beginning to find his encounters with Daciana were less fulfilling and enjoyable as they had been. She had stopped reaching into his mind long ago, and without the pleasure augmentation, the sex was as dull as the rest of his life had become.

With his new found freedom, he found that he could leave the castle unseen. He decided to return to the village that he had known as a boy, and found that it had changed a great deal.

They still lived in relative poverty to the life Durant led at the castle, but the streets smelled less foul and the village was now more of a town.

The countess had appointed a mayor to act as her representative in the village, and ensured that there were stories about the wealthy family in the castle, of sons and daughters, of weddings, births and deaths, that would belay any rumours of an ageless countess and her boy toy.

The girls in the village all seemed to share the same dream - of meeting the son of the countess and being whisked away to the castle as his wife.

This dream gave Durant a great scope to hunt the young virgins in the village and create his own brood. He took great pleasure in courting the young women, seducing them slowly, making them fall in love with him without affecting their minds.

He charmed them and brought them to the point where they would do anything for him. When he finally then took them to the castle he would marry the girls and live out a few years with them as his young brides before he would enthral them and make them his slaves.

He would tell the mayor that they had died in child birth, fell ill with whatever plague or disease was sweeping the land or that the son and his bride had departed for the lands the family owned in other parts of the country.

There was never any fuss, or scandal. No mobs came to the castle door baying for his blood, and so he continued, living life after life with the women he met. Playing games with their lives, causing them to love him and taking pleasure in the deception.

He was not sure he could even feel love any longer as his soul seemed to drift further from him with every drop of blood he drank and every life he took.

And Daciana was so wrapped up in her own thoughts, her own life, that she had no idea of what Durant was doing.

CHAPTER 5

Calista was a girl that had no illusions that life was hard. She had spent the first years of her life surrounded by love, not wealth, but she was cared for.

Until the plague came.

Her parents were amongst the first to be taken by the illness and when Calista was unscathed, people began to talk of her as though she was a witch, or worse, cursed.

She was soon ostracised by the people that had once been so kind to her. By the time she was sixteen, it was clear that she would never find peace if she stayed in the village of her birth.

So she packed her belongings and made her way to the town that lay beneath the castle of the countess.

The family had watched over the lands that Calista knew for generations, and it was in that castle that she would try to find work.

Calista was not afraid of hard work, and she knew that once under the protection of the family of the countess, she would not be thought of so poorly.

When she arrived in the town, she went to the inn to ask about the castle, and was told stories about the sons of the family who were often seen in the town. Of all the girls from the village that had been married and made the next countess.

Calista had no interest in trying to force the son of the countess to fall in love with her. Instead she pressed about working at the castle, but there was little that anyone could tell her, save from visiting the castle to ask the butler for employment.

She decided to eat at the inn before she made her way to the castle, but the night was drawing in, and the innkeeper suggested that she wait until morning, as there were rumours of wolves roaming the road between the town and the castle, looking for unsuspecting travellers to feast upon.

She had no one to explain to her how vulnerable a young woman travelling alone was, and the eyes of the men at the inn watched her every movement. Calista ate alone, feeling ever more uncomfortable under the gaze of the men at neighbouring tables, a sensation that was only changed by the opening of the door of the inn and a blast of cold air causing a shiver to run up her spine.

Durant felt something tugging at his soul. It was a feeling he had not felt before, and had been certain that he would never be able feel as he had forfeited such a luxury when he had accepted Daciana's offer of immortality.

But, all the same, there was a tug at his soul that

caused him to stir from his bed. It had been two months since he had roused from his slumber. His last wife had been buried for six months after dying trying to give birth to Durant's child.

No woman had survived the process but it was an easy way for Durant to dispose of the women without raising suspicion. Though the excuse could only be used once in every three wives.

Daciana had tolerated his fetish for living a relatively normal life with these women, though she still made him come to her bed and pleasure her.

But the moment the women died, she lost interest in her toy again until he found a new woman. She had far greater concerns and ambitions that spending an eternity in a swirling orgy of lust and perversion with Durant. But she was certain to remind him of his place in the castle and who his mistress was once he was married.

Durant found that he had no great ambition, no

desire for anything but a simple life, or at least playing at being the ideal husband whilst enthralling his wives and wielding his power over them.

It was more than enough for him, but once his wife was dead, he felt no need to do anything but sleep for months at a time. He rested, conserving his strength and needing nothing until he was awoken.

It also helped for the passage of time between his wives. But he had awaken much earlier than he would normally have done so.

He felt confused at the sensation that had caused him to wake and he wandered over to the window to try and make sense of it.

The tug was coming from the town below the castle, and he knew that the only way he would be able to make sense of it was to go out into the night to discover the source.

It did not take long for him to emerge into the cold night air, and make his way down the road. The wolves that guarded the road lifted their heads as their master went by, and then went back to lying in wait.

They were the beasts that guarded the thresholds, protection for the vampires whilst the slept and a deterrent for those that became too interested in the castle and its occupants.

As long as humans were in the company of either Durant or Daciana, they would not be harmed by the wolves.

As Durant made his way to the town, the tug on his soul grew stronger, until he found that the source was coming from the inn that lay at the centre of the town.

He threw open the doors without ceremony and searched the room. His eyes fell upon Calista's back and he knew at once that this woman was causing the tug on his soul, that out of every creature that had ever and would ever walk the earth, this woman was the other half of his heart, his fated mate and he had to possess her.

Calista felt Durant's eyes upon her and her heart skipped a beat. She turned slowly in her chair to look at the man who was staring at her, and the moment she looked into his eyes, she knew that she would never truly ever be able to escape the man that stood there.

"Your grace! What an honour!" the innkeeper stammered as he fell over himself trying to reach Durant.

"Thank you, I will be dining with my friend here," Durant said, gesturing at Calista.

"Oh, she is here as your guest. My apologies, I will see to your every need at once," the innkeeper said and disappeared into the back room.

The men in the room grumbled and turned their eyes away from Calista, all save for one man who stood and walked over to Calista's table.

He looked down at the woman before he reached out to grab her arm, intending to take her from the inn.

But before his fingers could ever graze her skin, he felt Durant's hand gripping his wrist and an intense feeling of fear gripped the man in the pit of his stomach.

"Your grace, please excuse our young friend," one of the men apologised and tried to extricate the young man from Durant's grasp.

"Your friend should learn that a woman is not his property to seize when he feels like it," Durant growled and Calista felt a smile curl at the corner of her mouth.

"Yes, your grace, of course," the man said as Durant released the wrist of the young man and allowed his friends to lead him away.

"Do you object to company?" Durant asked as he sat down opposite Calista and was able to look at her properly for the first time.

Beauty truly is in the eye of the beholder, and though Calista was attractive, she knew she was not the most beautiful woman that had ever lived. But to

Durant she truly was the most beautiful creature he had ever seen,

Her eyes were the clearest blue and made him feel like he was falling into them as he stared at her. Her lips were more inviting than anything he had ever known. Her hair was black and fell loose about her shoulders, long and lustrous, and Durant longed to run his fingers through it.

"No, I welcome it, sir," Calista replied politely and Durant felt his spirit soar as he heard her voice for the first time. Her mere presence was awakening feelings and emotions that he thought were long dead. If his heart could beat, he knew that it would threatening to escape his chest at this very moment.

And though he knew his own heart could not beat, he could hear hers. It was beating as fast as his would have been, and he knew that he was not alone in the feelings he was experiencing.

"My name is Durant, my mother is the countess

of the these lands and though I have no official title, I am known as the duke," Durant introduced himself as he settled himself into his chair.

"My name is Calista, I have no surname. I once did, but I left it behind me when I left my home. It is a name that has only brought me pain and suffering," she explained. She did not know why she was so willingly telling this man so much about herself, especially things she wanted to forget.

He was a handsome man, his looks were so striking, Calista was certain that she had never seen a man that looked so perfect before in her life.

His hair was a stunning blonde that seemed to shine in the light of the inn. His eyes were brown, so dark they were almost black and they called to her as she gazed at him. Their power was hypnotic that she felt that a single word from his mouth would make her follow him anywhere.

His chiselled chin and high cheek bones looked

as though her had been forged from the finest marble by the most skilled sculptor, and his smile was so disarming that the sight of it made Calista understood, for the first time, the urge in women to swoon and faint in the presence of certain men.

Her heart was beating so loudly in her chest she feared that he would here it and know how helpless she was before him.

"Then we shall leave that name in your past, and look to the future," Durant smiled. Calista had to close her eyes for a second as she felt dizzy in his presence and his smile had made her almost certain she would pass out. "Are you quite well?" Durant asked with concern in his voice.

"I am well, thank you," Calista smiled and opened her eyes, only to find that Durant was knelt beside her with a look of concern on his face.

"I fear you may need to rest. You have been travelling, yes?" Durant said as he offered her his arm and reached into his pocket to pull out a small pile of gold coins to pay the innkeeper with.

"I have, sir," Calista replied, glad to have such an excuse to hide the effect the man was having on her.

"Allow me to accompany you to your home or lodgings," Durant said as he helped her to her feet. The touch of her hand in his threatened to overwhelm him. The great beast in the pit of his stomach was bidding him to satisfy the basest of all his desires in front of all those in the inn.

"I am staying here, sir. I am in need of work and was coming to the castle in the morning to seek employment," Calista explained as she felt her head swim and her knees buckle in his presence.

Durant was quick to catch her and with one arm around her waist, he held her body against his. The scent of her skin was intoxicating and for the briefest moment he nearly forgot himself, his lips pressing against her neck, ready to feed.

"That will not do. This place is not safe for you to stay in. I will take you to the castle tonight where you can rest," Durant whispered in her ear and swept Calista off her feet, so that he was carrying her in his arms.

The innkeeper had returned to find the duke departing, gold piled on the table.

"Send the lady's baggage to the castle at first light," Durant instructed, and the innkeeper tugged at his forelock before he scurried to scoop up the gold from the table.

CHAPTER 6

Calista did not know how she came to be in the bed that she awoke in, but she knew that she must be at the castle.

The last thing she could remember was being picked up in the arms of Durant before she had passed out.

Sunlight was streaming through the window in her room and her bags from the inn lay at the foot of her bed.

She did not know how much time had passed, but there was a tray of food next to her bed that looked as though it had been placed there within the last half hour.

She ate the food gratefully, though found it odd that she was alone in the room, and that no one had come to wake her.

She felt Durant was close by and the thought of him made her soul ache for his presence. Calista wondered where he was and why he was not there with her, and then shook her head at such a ridiculous thought.

He did not belong to her and he had merely brought her to the castle where she sought to work. He was not under any obligation to her.

She lay back against the pillows once she had finished eating and sighed to herself. She did not feel she could explore the castle without her host to accompany her, so she decided all she could do was wait.

She closed her eyes and thought back over her first meeting with Durant and could not help but smile.

The door to her room opened quietly and one of the maids stole into the room to gather her tray and close the curtains. Calista was so lost in her thoughts of the previous night she did not notice the presence of the maid.

As soon as the curtain was closed, Durant stole into the room, wiping the smallest flecks of blood from the corners of his mouth as he did so.

He had fed well on one of the younger maids who was only too willing to give herself to her master. Simply allowing Durant to feed caused her to reach realms of ecstasy that most other women could only dream of.

Durant knew that the young maid would not last for more than a year before she was spent, but that was all he needed.

He would not waste any time in seducing Calista and ensnaring her heart.

"You ate well?" he asked, causing Calista to jump slightly as she opened her eyes and saw the man standing over her.

"I did, thank you, sir," Calista replied as she tried to extricate herself from the sheets and blankets on the bed so that she might stand in his presence, but Durant moved to sit on the edge of the bed, forcing her to remain in it.

"Please, call me Durant, my lady," he replied and Calista blushed.

"If it pleases you, sir, but I came to be a maid in this great house. How can I work here and be on such easy terms with my master?" Calista asked. As the word master escaped her lips, she felt dizzy again, and Durant felt a surge of desire for her.

"You will not be a maid in this house," Durant said softly as he reached out for her hand.

"No?" Calista asked, a desperate fear suddenly clutching at her heart.

"No. I could not have such a rare beauty as yours wasted in drudgery," Durant replied as he leaned closer to her.

"Then what is to become of me?" Calista asked looking up at Durant with doeful eyes.

"What does your heart say?" Durant whispered as he stroked her cheek gently.

Calista felt her heart pounding in her chest and the desire to kiss Durant was so intense that she could not resist her urges.

She reached out and grabbed Durant by the neck, pulling him close to her, the instant their lips met, she knew that there would be no other man for her.

Durant felt the ferocious passion behind her kiss, the surprise he felt at her sudden embrace was soon overcome by his own need for the woman he knew was his fated mate.

He kissed her back with equal passion, pushing her back against the pillows on the bed so that he could climb on top of her.

Calista felt his body pressing down on hers and for the slightest moment she resisted. Her entire upbringing had told her that she should not give her virtue up so easily, but her desire for purity was soon extinguished by the need she had for Durant's body.

She felt Durant pressing himself against her, grinding slowly but firmly as they kissed.

"Am I to be your whore?" Calista asked as she managed to part their lips for a moment. Durant felt himself surge at the thought of Calista as his whore, and he felt her pulse quicken as she asked.

"Do you wish to be my whore? My slut?" he whispered in her ear and Calista could not help but let out a moan.

"I will be whatever my master wishes me to be," Calista replied and Durant smiled down at her with a greedy look of desire on his face.

She felt his hands moving slowly down her body, until they reached the bottom of her nightdress. He paused for a moment, waiting for her to tell him to stop, but she did not. Instead, Calista reached down and began to pull off the white shift she wore, slowly revealing her pale and perfect body that had been hidden beneath it.

Durant stepped off the bed and looked at the woman lying in the bed before him. She looked up at him expectantly, but when he did not disrobe, Calista slipped off the bed and began to undress Durant.

He smiled at her willingness and cupped her breasts with his firm hands as her fingers pulled at the ties on his trousers,

She could see his cock pressing against the fabric of his trousers, trying to escape the prison it was contained within.

As the final tie was undone, Durant seized hold of her neck and waist and pulled her against his naked body, kissing her more desperately than before.

Calista kissed him back, losing herself completely in the desire and lust she felt for him. She was about to pull him back to the bed, when she felt Durant pushing her away from it. He kept pushing her backwards until Calista felt herself collide with the wall.

Durant pressed himself against her so firmly she could not help but moan softly. He reached down and pushed his hand roughly between her legs, forcing them apart.

She had never known the touch of a man before, so every sensation was new to her, She felt his fingers slowly rubbing against her clit, causing her to gasp and groan with pleasure,

Durant watched her reactions with a smile on his face.

"More?" he whispered to her.

"Yes, master, please," Calista begged.

"Good girl," he replied as he slipped his fingers lower, slipping them inside her wet pussy. Calista grabbed at Durant's shoulders, digging her fingernails into his skin as she felt new and exciting waves of pleasure. She bit her lip to keep herself from screaming.

"More?" he asked again, his breathing laboured

with his need to fuck her.

"Please, master," Calista replied and Durant pulled back his fingers, and used both hands to grab hold of Calista's butt cheeks and lifted her off her feet,

She wrapped her legs around his waist without a single thought, Durant pinning her against the wall at the perfect height for penetration.

Calista screamed as Durant thrust himself inside her, his big, hard cock, causing her equal realms of pleasure and pain. His hands no longer held her ass, but had moved up her body to her shoulders, wrapping around behind them so that he could pull her down onto his cock as he thrust up inside her.

Calista was powerless within his strong arms, but she had no desire to escape him, she wanted him, she revelled in the pleasure and pain he was causing in her.

Durant was so lost in his need for her that he had lost all sense of gentleness. Instead, he fucked her harder and harder, he wanted to make her scream louder and louder, each scream urging him to keep going.

Her legs squeezed hard around his waist, her arms around his own shoulders, their bodies so closely entwined that Durant could not help but bury his face in her neck. He could feel her heart racing, hear her blood coursing through her body, until he could resist the desire to feed no longer.

Calista cried out with shock as she felt his fangs piercing the white flesh of her neck, but in that pain there was more pleasure than she had ever experienced, and even more so as he drank from her.

She did not question what was happening, her mind was so consumed with lust for Durant she did not care what he was.

"More, master, more," she begged as she grabbed at his hair, pushing his head even harder into her neck.

Durant had never known any blood to taste as Calista's did. It was like a drug, once he had tasted it, he could not stop feeding, nor could he stop fucking her, but the more he fed, the weaker her grasp on his body became.

She was on the verge of losing conciousness when Durant realised he had drunk too much. Her legs were still wrapped around his body but the pressure they had been applying had gone.

He pulled her body away from the wall and lowered her back the ground.

"Master?" she asked in confusion, sounding disappointed that Durant had stopped.

"I want you on the bed," he whispered in her ear, and Calista smiled. With his arm around her waist, pressing her body against his as they moved, her steered her to the bed, pushing her slowly down.

He pinned her down with one hand, holding her hands above her head as she writhed willingly beneath him.

Calista reached up and pulled his head towards hers, kissing him as firmly as she could.

"Tell me what you want," Durant said softly as he rest his forehead upon hers.

"I want you, all of you," Calista replied.

Durant smiled and kissed her gently and reached down to guide his throbbing member into her warm, soft pussy.

He slowly thrust himself into her, deep and hard, letting her feel every inch of him. He let the rhythm build, her body responding to each thrust of his. He fucked her harder and harder, each thrust causing her to moan and scream louder and louder until she passed out from the pleasure.

He smiled down at her, satisfied that he had given her what she wanted. He kept fucking her, until he came deep inside of her, then rolled to lie beside her on the bed, waiting for her to regain conciousness.

Calista did not know how long she had been out, but she knew she was not alone. She turned her head to see Durant sleeping beside her. She felt weak and dizzy from the experience, but she knew that she wanted more.

CHAPTER 7

For three days, Durant did not leave her side. When they were not lost in throes of passion for one another, they slept and talked.

Durant had resisted the urge to enthral Calista. He had not reached into her mind once as he wanted her to love him and need him, as he loved and needed her.

Instead he used everything he had learn from Daciana about sex to pleasure Calista and increase her desire for him without resorting to his vampiric powers.

He fucked her until she was so tired she could not help but sleep through the day and then the two would spend their nights in passionate throes. He made sure that she ate well and had plenty of foods filled with iron.

He resisted feeding from her again until she had recovered her strength, and instead had goblets of blood brought from the kitchen for him to feed from.

Durant knew that Daciana would not notice his absence, until it suited her. But what he did not account for was the loyalty of her own thralls.

There were plenty among their number that wished to become vampires, to take their place at her side as her equal, not simply her playthings that she used when she was bored or stressed.

One in particular knew from experience that his looks would soon fade and so would his usefulness to his mistress.

Argo had been sixteen when he had first met the countess and willingly come to the castle to serve her. He had not needed to be enthralled for many years. His devotion to her had been absolute but his jealousy, watching the countess take part in orgies with her thralls as her pet Durant watched had caused him to lash out at the others.

Daciana had not been willing to kill him as he was a good worker in her household, but she had needed to control him and so she had enthralled him.

It had not taken much, and at times, the countess wondered why she had bothered, but the lack of jealous outbursts she had to contend with was far better than the headache-causing drama.

Argo had retained more of his sense than most thralls as he had already been so devoted to his mistress there was minimal damage to his mind.

Those who fought against being enthralled were the ones who were left as mindless slaves. Daciana had often found it amusing that this was the case, and had, more than once, provoked a potential thrall so that they would resist, just so she could have the pleasure of breaking their minds entirely.

Argo had become suspicious that he had not seen Durant for two days. Normally he would leave the castle when in search of a new bride, and present the girl to Daciana for approval once he found her. But as this normal routine had been interrupted, the thrall had become curious about what exactly Durant was doing.

He watched the maids that took food and blood to his rooms, and at midday, when he knew Durant would be asleep, Argo crept into the vampire's room to discover the girl in his bed.

He thought about waking her, but instead went to question Durant's thralls and soon discovered all that Durant had been up to.

Argo had not decided what he would do with the information until he came into the presence of Daciana that evening.

The countess was lovely as ever, the most beautiful creature that Argo had ever laid his eyes upon and the mere sight of her made him hungry for her touch.

He was not thirty-seven, and though still strong

and handsome, he was called to the countess' bed less and less now in favour of younger meat.

As he stood before her, he could see the disinterest in her face. He was there now, not as an object of desire but as a beast of burden, and even as a thrall, he could not bear to be thought of as such.

"Mistress, I have distressing news to report," Argo said with desperation.

"Oh?" Daciana asked, sounding bored before the conversation had even begun.

"It is about Durant. He has taken a lover without your approval," Argo began and the countess looked up at him with an expression of disbelief.

She struggled not to laugh in Argo's face as he stood there and she replied,

"And why should that bother me?"

"Because one of his thralls heard him call this girl his fated mate," Argo replied. The words had the intended effect on Daciana as her expression changed from one of mirth to boiling rage.

"What?" she asked, her anger barely in check.

"His fated mate," Argo repeated.

"Of all the ungrateful," Daciana began as she advanced on Argo. He did not understand what was happening and when he felt the teeth of his mistress plunge into his neck, for the briefest moment there was pure ecstasy.

But the horror of his mistake became apparent all too soon. Rather than the images in his mind that he was used to when intimate with his mistress, there were now images of torture and brutality.

His mind became consumed by fear of her rage, and he soon realised he was screaming in pain as the countess tore his body to pieces.

When Argo lay dead about her, she cried out in frustration and went in search of Durant's thralls. When they confirmed Argo's story, it was all she could do not to kill the two girls on the spot.

Daciana withdrew to her study and began to plot. It had been one thing, letting Durant play house and indulge his human fantasies, but it was quite another for him to find someone to replace her.

She was his mate. He belonged to her for all eternity. It was the bargain they had struck and with all his games of happy families, he had remained true to his word.

Now he had broken it.

After two days of thinking, she had a plan. She would kill the girl that had usurped her and she would make Durant pay for his betrayal. But this castle was not the venue for such revenge.

She summoned all of her thralls to her bed chamber that night and one-by-one she drained the life from them in an orgy of sex, bloodlust, and rage.

She left only her oldest and most trusted thrall alive as he would remain in guardianship of the castle, his own son ready to take over his father's post should he die at it.

It had been that way for centuries.

The thralls that died in her bed that night did not know the pain and terror that Argo had felt, instead their deaths were merciful. All died knowing only the pleasure of their mistress' bed.

Daciana ordered her remaining thrall to instruct Durant's thralls to shut up the castle, and pass word that her own thralls had gone on ahead to prepare their other home for their arrival.

She did not need the girls to fear her yet. That would come in time, and she did not need Durant alerted to her knowledge of his fated mate.

CHAPTER 8

When Durant awoke that night, he found the castle in disarray.

"What is going on?" he demanded of one of his thralls.

"The mistress has ordered the castle shut up and for all to be ready to depart by midnight," the thrall replied to her master.

Durant was furious with Daciana for forcing the move, if only because it made him leave the bed of Calista. They would not be able to be together again until they reached their other castle and Daciana was entrenched there in her work.

But he knew better than to go and speak to the woman about it. She was not going to change whatever plans she had made upon Durant's say so.

He had expected that a move would come soon.

They often did after the death of one of his wives. But he also was normally given some form of notice that this was happening.

The lack of warning did not alarm him, merely caused him to feel resentful towards his sire.

Rather than waste time arguing, he prepared for the journey and warned Calista about what was about to happen.

Calista was glad of the rest. Three nights of nothing but sex had been quite exhausting, and though she had enjoyed it, the rest was something she was looking forward to.

Two carriages were prepared for the vampires to travel in, each with blacked out windows and heavy curtains to draw over the cracks in the doors.

Daciana and Durant would travel one in each coach and when they stopped at inns and towns along the journey they would return to their carriages before morning to sleep.

The thralls of Durant were not permitted to travel in the carriages, instead they were all put into a cart which was one of six. The other five carts housed the belongings of the countess and her pet, and they followed behind the two carriages along the road.

Men were hired to protect the grand train and were paid well so that none of them would think of stealing from Daciana.

The journey was set to take six days to complete as long as the weather did not turn.

Durant made sure that plenty of cloaks and furs were packed into the cart for his thralls to wear if the weather turned. Not just for Calista's sake, but so that he did not lose any of his other thralls as well.

Durant and Daciana did not allow anyone to enter the carriages during the daylight hours, for fear that they would be exposed to sunlight and turn to dust.

Calista was not sure would be able to spend so

much time away from Durant, but she knew that Daciana made the rules and she would have to obey them.

Even when the carts stopped at the inns, the thralls were not permitted into the rooms of their master and mistress. They slept in the carts in the stables with only the furs that Durant had provided to keep them warm.

In the castle, the thralls were used to keeping nocturnal hours, but when travelling, being exposed to the sun made it impossible for them to sleep. On the first night of their journey, all of the thralls were so exhausted that they did not touch the food that was brought out to them by the innkeeper's daughter.

They slept through until just before the first light of morning. As the stable boys hurried around, fixing the horses to their traces, and Durant and Daciana appeared from within the confines of the inn, Calista realised that there was one of their number missing.

A young thrall, a girl named Marissa, was not in the cart and nobody had seen her. Calista was worried and begged Daciana to delay their departure so that she could search for the missing girl, but Daciana had refused.

"The girl was foolish enough to wander off, then she deserves to be left behind. We shall not be delayed by those that get lost," Daciana had snapped and the convoy had lurched onwards with one missing from the thralls number.

On the second night, three of the maids went missing. With three of their number vanished, Durant insisted that a search for the girls be held before they left the inn the next morning. Their bodies were found not far from the inn, all torn apart, as though they had been set upon by wolves.

On the third night, the male thralls were all slaughtered in their carriage. Fear spread amongst the remaining three female thralls, and the mercenaries that

Daciana had hired demanded a pay increase for the risks they faced.

On the fourth night, the mercenaries were killed and the other female thrall and the last of the maids. Only Calista and the drivers remained.

Durant feared for her safety and insisted that a room in the inn be given to her and another to their drivers. Daciana did not refuse his request, but the idea of paying for a room for the help clearly rankled at her soul.

Calista climbed into bed that night, terrified of the slightest movement. Her heart pounded in her chest and she was almost too terrified to sleep.

A creak in the hallway caused her to sit bolt-upright in bed. She did not see Daciana enter, but knew that danger was close at hand. Every fibre of her being told her to scream, to run, to be as far from this place as she could, but fear rooted her to her bed.

"You are to blame," Daciana said.

"Excuse me?" Calista stuttered.

"You are to blame for all of this. You are the last because I want to make you suffer for all that you have taken from me. I will take my time destroying you, tearing your flesh from your bones, and I will make him watch. He will be powerless to stop me, and you will both know the meaning of true pain. He will watch your life seeping away, but before you die, I will make you watch as I kill him too. You shall be parted forever, not even in death can you ever reunite. You shall both die and I shall endure this betrayal," Daciana hissed in her ear.

Calista screwed up her eyes tightly and tried not to panic, but at the height of her fear, Daciana vanished. The fear ebbed away and Calista was left to weep in her bed.

<u>CHAPTER 9</u>

The convoy was ready to travel the next morning and it lurched on its journey. At around midday, the drivers stopped to eat and shared their meagre meal with Calista.

She had not decided what she could do, if anything against the might of Daciana. She did not know if there was anywhere she could run, and she knew that if they arrived at the castle that she and Durant would both be dead before the sunrise.

The only thing she could think of was to convince the drivers to set fire to Daciana's carriage and leave it to burn with her inside. But she did not think she could persuade the men to murder their employer.

Instead, she decided to send the drivers all on ahead.

"I will drive my mistress' carriage, to ensure it

reaches the castle safely. You are to deliver the rest of the convoy to the castle and then leave. You are dismissed," Calista said firmly, and the drivers did not argue.

There was something about the countess that made them feel nervous and uncomfortable, to be able to complete their mission and leave without further contact with Daciana was the best outcome they could hope for.

When the drivers were out of sight, Calista unhooked the horses from their traces and tied them to a tree a good distance from where the carriage stood. She had a sliver of flint that she had found and a pile of broken twigs, sticks and dried bracken that she placed under on of the carriage wheels.

It took an hour for her to build the small fire and set it alight. When she was certain that the carriage was ablaze, Calista retrieved the horses and made to catch up to the convoy.

Calista did not believe that fire could destroy the countess, and that she would be coming to claim her revenge against Calista and Durant as soon as she possibly could.

The drivers had safely delivered Durant and the treasury of the countess to her castle, but instead of going to join Durant, Calista went to speak with the local priest about the destruction of evil.

The priest was surprised by the conversation topic, but was more than happy to listen to the tale that Calista had to tell. He listened to all that Calista had seen of Daciana, the business with the thralls and how they had met their ends.

His brow grew ever more furrowed as she described the countess, but he did not speak a word until she was finished. When she was done, the priest looked at her gravely and reached into his pocket.

"Here, my child, you will need this," he pressed a vial into her hand.

"What is it?" Calista frowned.

"It is holy water. It will help protect you. We shall need more than this though. What you have told me of is pure evil, and it is not something I can allow to endure. I will need to go now and speak with others of my order. There is a great deal I must do before this evil arrives at our doors. I will make my preparations and come to the castle before nightfall. If there is any delay, I will send some of the brothers to fetch you back here. You will be safe within these walls from the reach of her evil if we cannot be ready before she descends on this place," the priest said earnestly. Calista nodded her agreement and made her way back to the castle.

Durant was safely within the castle walls and out of the glare of the blinding day. He was worried when

Calista was not there, but the butler assured him that Calista would return shortly.

Durant paced the castle and was surprised to find that Daciana had not yet arrived. He missed the presence of his other thralls, not from any form of affection towards them, but his boredom caused him to feel hungry, and there was nothing but the butler to feed upon in the castle.

When Calista finally returned to the castle, it took all of Durant's restraint to not drain every last drop of blood from the woman.

Seeing him driven to distraction by hunger, she allowed him to feed without expecting anything in return. But Durant did not want her to simply be his food source.

He slowly removed her clothing from her, allowing his fingers to explore every inch of her skin, his gentle touch arousing her, teasing her, causing her to be helpless before him.

He stood behind her and bit down hard on the soft curve of her neck, causing Calista to cry out slightly in a mixture of surprise, pain and pleasure.

Durant pulled her close, one arm wrapped across her chest holding her breast, squeezing it as he drank deeply from her. His other hand reached down between her legs, his fingers slipping between her pussy lips and inside her.

He drank until he felt her climax, her wet pussy dripping down her legs, then spinning her around, he dropped to his knees and began to lick up every last drop of the juices coming from between her legs.

He listened to her moan as his tongue pleasured her and waited for her to beg for more from him.

"Please, Durant, we must talk," Calista protested, despite her desire for him to fuck her.

"About what?" Durant asked as he rested his chin upon her belly.

"Daciana will be here soon. She is the one that

murdered all the thralls and she will see me dead too. She wants to make us both suffer because you have betrayed her heart, and I have tried to usurp her," Calista explained.

Durant frowned darkly.

"And she will leave me alive to suffer?"

"No, she is going to kill you too," Calista said as she knelt so that she was on the same level as Durant.

"I cannot raise a hand against her, she has made sure that those she sires cannot rise against her. I do not know how she has accomplished such a thing, but I cannot save you from her," Durant said sadly. He felt helpless for the first time since he had been turned.

"You do not need to. Trust me, I shall stop Daciana, and I will protect you," Calista promised. Durant looked confused at the determination of the woman who knelt before him.

He did not understand how she could be so calm in the face of all that Daciana could do to her and him, but he took some small solace in her serenity.

"What are you going to do?" Durant asked as he reached out and gently stroked Calista's face.

"I cannot tell you, but please, trust me," Calista said with a half-smile.

"I do trust you, and I love you. If I am capable of such things now," Durant sighed. Calista looked slightly shocked at the revelation, but once she had recovered from the momentary surprise, she smiled more broadly at him.

"I love you too," she admitted. "But I must get ready now. Stay here for now, Daciana will surely fetch you when she arrives, and she will expect that I have told you why she is coming. You should know that I set fire to her carriage with her inside it," Calista added almost as an afterthought.

Durant could not help but laugh at the revelation and how she announced such a terrible act with such disregard for it.

"There is far more to you than even I suspected," Durant grinned. "Be careful, my love. I do not like not knowing what will happen, but I will trust you and hope that you will be safe, at least for the moment."

Calista nodded and dressed herself quickly. She left Durant kneeling on the floor, wondering what he would do to pass the time before Daciana arrived. But Calista had other things to focus on.

<u>CHAPTER 10</u>

The night drew in faster than Calista expected it to, but the priest and his brothers arrived, ready to assist her. Calista couldn't help but feel nervous as her whole plan hinged on her being able to trigger the trap that was set.

She checked everything twice and then went to Durant. He was looking out of the window when she slipped through the door. The sun had set and he was looking, seemingly watching for Daciana's approach.

Calista wrapped her arms around him from behind and leant her head against his back.

"Come lie with me," Calista whispered. "I want her to believe we thought her dead and are not prepared for her reprisals."

Durant sighed and shook his head.

"Please be careful, she is far more dangerous than you know. Do not under estimate her," Durant warned her as he took her hands from around his waist and led her to the bed to lie down together.

Durant did not want to undress, but Calista insisted that it must look as though they had no cares but for each other.

For an hour they lay in the dark without saying a word. Neither of them knew what to say and did not want the final words they might share to be the wrong ones.

Calista lay reflecting on how she could love such a man as Durant in such a deep way having known him so short a time, but she could not help how she felt, nor how Durant felt either.

She closed her eyes and felt herself drifting off to sleep when the doors to the castle were flung open with a mighty crash.

Calista sat bolt upright in the bed, Durant beside her, holding her naked body closely to him. The two sat in silent terror as they listened to Daciana approaching.

Doors were flung open on each room as she seemed to be conducting a search for them.

The sound of her approaching, drawing ever closer, awoke a primal fear that gnawed at Calista's soul. She had never thought of the evil that she lived with until the priest had mentioned it. Her mind and body had both been consumed by lust, desire and a desperation to remain.

But now, as she trembled and her instincts bade her not to make a sound, she knew that the slightest mistake would certainly end in her death.

Her heart pounded in her chest and Durant could feel every emotion that poured through her body. He held her as tightly as he dared. He did not want to hurt her, but he could not let her go.

In all of his life, there had never been anything he truly cared for, anything he wanted to keep for himself, until he had met Calista, and now Daciana threatened to take that from him, as she had taken his life and his freedom.

Each crash of a door being ripped from it's hinges and cast aside told them how close Daciana was to finding them.

"Run, leave this place. I will find you," Durant whispered urgently, his fear overwhelming him and begging her to flee.

"It is too late to flee, too late to hide," Calista whispered back and kissed Durant passionately.

The door to the room was pulled away from the wall as though it weighed nothing and was tossed aside with a yell that seemed to come from the depths of hell itself.

"I have found you both, you traitorous dogs!" Daciana roared.

Durant did not dare open his eyes or stop kissing Calista. If this were to be the last time that they embraced, he would not be the one to end it.

Calista felt a rough hand grip her shoulder and

tear her away from Durant. She felt Durant's hands clawing at her body, trying to keep her close, but Daciana was too strong and his fingers merely left deep scratches over her body.

Durant cried out for Calista as she was ripped from his grasp and looked with rage on the figure of the woman he had endured for so long. But she was no longer the unnaturally beautiful countess he had spent years coming to resent.

Her perfect skin had become charred beyond all recognition. Her lips were shrivelled and cracked. Her hair was gone, burned to faint whispers of ash upon her scalp, and her eyes were now the colour of the fires of hell.

She was a monster, salivating for revenge.

Despite his need to protect Calista, his rage at Daciana for daring to harm her and his other thralls, he could not bring himself to attack.

Everything inside him told him to strike, to tear

her limb from limb, but when he attempted to move with murderous intent, his blood froze in his veins, paralysing him.

He could only watch in helpless terror as Daciana gripped Calista by the hair and dragged her from the room.

Calista screamed as her naked body was dragged over the rough stone floor, the wounds from Durant's fingers being added to by the sharp edges of the giant stones.

Durant rushed after them, though he could do nothing, he did not want to be out of sight of Calista.

Daciana tutted in scorn as she saw Durant scampering after them like a love-sick puppy.

"What did I ever see in you? You pathetic little worm," Daciana yelled as she threw Calista, like a rag doll, across the floor and used the back of her hand to knock Durant flat on his back.

The vampire cried out as he flew backwards into

the wall and landed hard in a heap on the floor. He had no way to defend himself against her, just as he could not attack her. He knew it was pointless to get up, but he could not simply lie down and admit defeat.

But Daciana did not need to waste time or energy on her progeny when Calista was still able to move.

She was already advancing across the floor towards the bleeding girl. Daciana would feed, but not until she had sufficiently punished her.

Durant resisted his own hunger. He knew that Calista was already weakened from her earlier loss of blood to him, and that losing much more would put her life in danger. Though blood loss was the least of her worries for the moment.

Daciana kicked the girl and sent her rolling further across the floor. She had dragged her to the grand hall. It was where the countess would hold audience with those that wished to petition her, but now it would be the place where she killed the two traitors in her midst and would be reminded of their purging every time she sat in the hall.

The thought of reliving her assured victory over the conniving pair distracted her for a moment, and that was all the distraction that Calista needed.

She crawled as fast as she could across the hall and grabbed at one of the tapestries. An instant later, arrows were unleashed from bows, the sound of the strings singing as they were released and the snap of the arrows slamming home echoed around the hall.

The brethren of the church had all lined the upper gallery and were now raining arrows down upon the countess as she stood in the centre of the room.

Daciana laughed, a hollow and cruel sound, at the feeble attempts of the priests.

"Foolish mortals. You have no idea whom it is you are dealing with," she scoffed, but as the words left her mouth, she felt a strange dizziness begin to overwhelm her. "What have you done?" she demanded as she fell to her knees.

"Child of darkness, you are nothing before the power of light. Our arrows have all been soaked in holy water and blessed by the bishop. These are our instruments of light and your darkness will fall in the face of them," the priest called out in a clear and thunderous voice.

Durant felt a chill run down his spine at the thought and did his best to shrink back into darkness, away from the avenging men of God.

"You will pay for this," Daciana snarled as she tried to stand again, but failed and dropped to her knees a second time.

"Now is your chance, child," the priest called out to Calista. She was unsteady on her feet, but she staggered forward with blurred vision as the priest threw something down to her from the gallery.

A wooden stick with a filed point landed with a

clatter not far from Calista. The priest had explained what needed to be done, according to the ancient texts, and though Calista had thought she was prepared to do what was necessary. She paused as the realisation of what was to come set in.

"Take it now, there is not much time," the priest urged, and Calista did as she was bade. She gripped the stick as firmly as she could and stabbed Daciana in the chest with it, piercing her heart.

Daciana cried out in pain, but it lasted only a moment as she exploded in a cloud of dust and ash. Calista coughed, and spluttered as she collapsed to the floor as the dust and ash settled.

Daciana was dead, gone and she was safe. The priests came down from the gallery and gave the naked girl a robe to cover herself with.

"You should come to the Abbey tonight. Your injuries must be treated and you need to rest. Does your paramour need assistance as well?" the priest asked.

"No, he was not harmed. He was locked in a room, but the butler will free him now," Calista assured the monks. The priest nodded and two of his brothers stepped forward with a litter to carry Calista upon.

CHAPTER 11

Calista spent several days with the monks, allowing her body to heal and her mind to recover from all that had transpired since she had met Durant.

She had begun to feel sick in the mornings and was assured that it was simply exhaustion. But Calista did not believe the brothers were right. In fact, she was certain she was pregnant. She did not understand how it was possible, but she knew that she carried Durant's baby.

When she was well enough to return to the castle, she did so with apprehension. Though she had seen Daciana explode before her into a cloud of ash and dust, there was a small doubt in her mind that felt she may have been tricked, and that by returning to the castle, she would be walking into Daciana's clutches.

But the countess was dead, and Durant was

eagerly awaiting her. He had not been able to visit Calista whilst she had been cloistered on holy ground, and instead he had watched her from afar.

He knew there was something she wanted to tell him the moment she walked into the castle, but he did not give her a moment to speak. He rush to her and took her in his arms. He kissed her, gently at first, but then more urgently.

Being with Durant again banished all doubts and fears that had plagued her dreams in the Abbey. She was with the man she loved, and her emotions for him overwhelmed her. She was lost in her desire for him, and it took no convincing for her to be lead by her lover into the depths of the castle.

He led her down spiralling staircases into what appeared to be the dungeon. There were rows and rows of cells that lined the corridor they walked down, and Calista felt her chest tighten with fear.

Durant did not offer her any explanation for

where they were going, and it was only her love and trust in him that kept her from pulling away from him.

He led her to a room with a rack and chains, and once she was safely in the cell with him, he turned and closed the door.

"Do not fear, it is not locked yet. Depending on your answer, I will either open the door or lock it," Durant said, but though his tone was calm and soothing, it did nothing to alleviate her fears.

"Why have you brought me here?" Calista asked, her voice catching in her throat.

"Peace, my love, peace," Durant soothed as he took her face in his hands and kissed her gently. "I have something to offer you."

"Offer me?" Calista frowned.

"A gift. Eternal life at my side," Durant said with a smile that was entirely disarming.

"You would make me into one of you?" Calista said.

"Yes, but not just making you one of me, but giving you strength, speed, stamina, life at my side and love that never ends," Durant said.

"Before I answer, I am with child. I carry your child within me. I do not know how, but you should know, if that affects the gift you offer," Calista said.

"You carry my child?" Durant asked with surprise. "That is wonderful news! I have lost many wives and children in childbirth, but they were not given the gift I now offer to you. It may only be possible for our child to be born if you accept this gift," he explained with delight.

"Then I accept," Calista said. "Why did you bring me to this awful room to ask me?"

Durant did not reply at once but moved to the door and locked it.

"The change is not an easy one. I was close to death when I was given this gift, so my change was much simpler than most. There is a risk, a risk that if you are not strong enough, you will lose your mind to the dark impulses and hunger, that you will become a mindless killer that must be put down. Long ago, those of our kind learnt to chain up those that are being given this gift. Not only to protect ourselves, but them as well," Durant explained.

"What will happen?" Calista asked.

"I will chain you to this rack. Then I shall feed until you are almost at the point of death, I shall bring you to the highest point of ecstasy that you can imagine, and then you will drink from this chalice. It contains my blood and the blood of those lords that came before me. The strength of our kind is in this chalice. Our strength will then become yours. If you possess the strength to master our baser nature, you will be by my side forever. If you do not, I will not let you suffer," Durant assured her.

"Very well. I give myself to you and this gift, for all eternity and can only pray that we shall spend eternity as one. But should I fail, know that I love you," Calista said and kissed Durant.

EPILOGUE

Lucian shook his head and brought himself back to the present. He had lived for hundreds of years now and was by no means the pathetic child who needed fairy tales for hope of a better life.

He often wondered if that story had remained with him because it had been the last vestige of a life that was twice dead to him, the concepts of love, devotion and desire where extremely human and far removed from him. But he did think, on occasion, that there was something more to his connection with the story than he knew.

He had often heard his vampiric father talk of fated mates, of a destiny and love that one cannot escape. There had been vampires drawn to humans, to rival clans and even to other shifter races, but for Lucian Dark there had been nothing. No woman had ever reached out to claim his cold dark heart, and after so many centuries, he couldn't imagine anything as laughable as fated mate appearing when he least expected it.

He sighed to himself and stared down at the street below. There were human cattle roaming the streets, blissfully unaware of the hunter that watched them from above. He debated whether he would go down and feed tonight or have one of the thralls brought up from the dungeon of the great tower. They were always so eager to please, to do whatever they could to make their master happy. But there was no pleasure it it for him.

"Are you going out tonight?" a voice asked from behind him.

"I think I must, Harry," Lucian replied to his companion.

Harry was a young vampire, the newest addition to Lucian's coven. He was handsome, and only a few decades into his life as a creature of the night. He was still charming, in a disarming way, and had at least a passing connection to the world still that allowed him to teach the others all they needed to know about the outside world. Young blood was vital to bring in to the family to keep the older vampires from becoming woefully out of touch.

"Excellent, I know exactly where we should go," Harry beamed. Lucian thought about protesting but it was not often that Harry was able to take his lord out hunting and it seemed cruel to deny him the opportunity now.

"Lead on then," Lucian replied.

"Not before you change into something a little more modern. The 17th century look plays well for a brooding vampire lord on his throne, but looks more like fancy dress or a cheap costume to ladies down there," Harry said with a slight smirk.

"Dress me as you will," Lucian said with a wave

of his hand and Harry scampered off, returning moments later with an exquisitely tailored suit and shirt in hand.

"Saville Row?" Lucian asked with a raised eyebrow.

"Of course," Harry smiled. Though Harry was an American boy through and through, Lucian had been raised in England and as such, Harry knew there were certain things that his master appreciated, and Saville Row was one of them.

"Very well," Lucian said without emotion. He took the offered suit and cast one more look down at the street below. Something was down there, something reaching out to him.

He changed quickly and the two men made their way down the stairs to the entrance to Dark Tower. The tower stood as a beacon to many business minds in the city, it was the heart of Lucian's financial empire that kept the people of this place employed and his own wealth at a more than healthy level.

Lucian had a reputation as a workaholic so it was never unusual for him to be seen outside at all. Meetings were always held in his tower and his aversion to light was explained away by him suffering from ocular migraines triggered by an excess of light.

As he and Harry walked down the street many eyes turned towards them. Most men on the street were dressed in casual wear, nothing special and something that marked them as unsuitable for many of the women that were looking for a man to take care of them.

The men that were dressed in suits were bankers with an attitude to match, something that was off putting to all but those with trophy spouse ambitions. Lucian thought to himself that as abhorrent as their behaviour was, they would have to add one of them to their number soon. But that was not what was calling to him tonight.

Harry led the way through the mass of people

until they reached the door to a bar that sat on one of the busiest intersections in the city.

"This is where you come to hunt?" Lucian asked in a low voice.

"It is, you might be surprised," Harry smiled. He pushed open the door and revealed a world of alcohol and desperation. The air was rank with the need to belong to something, anything, of the need to escape from the confines of pathetic and humdrum lives.

"I see," Lucian grinned.

"Simone is over there," Harry pointed and began to push his way through the people. Simone was one of Lucian's thralls. A woman who was not only desperately in love with Lucian but desperate to be one of his coven, more than a thrall, but a fully fledge vampire. She was not a good candidate though, and Lucian had never risked unleashing more ferals on the world.

When vampires turned a mere mortal to their

kind there were two possible outcomes - the birth of a new vampire or the corruption of their creation into a mindless feral monster that was a threat to all life. These beasts were only interested in blood, no matter where it came from and it was the responsibility of all shifters to put an end to these monsters.

Lucian did not follow Harry. He stood rooted to the spot as he surveyed the room. Whatever had been calling to him on his balcony, was in this room. At first he thought it might be the thrill of seducing several prey, of bringing men and women alike back to his tower for a great feast that had not been done since Queen Victoria had ruled the British Empire. But then he realised there was something else in this bar, something that didn't belong in such a place.

He cast his eye, searching with every instinct until he found it. Two women were sat at a table together. They were laughing and joking, talking of nothing and everything, but they did not reek of the same pitiably emotions that the others did. They were both confident, self-assured, and did not belong here.

Lucian's mouth curled at the corner as he analysed the two women. They were lean and strong, trained to fit in but to be guarded. Vampire Hunters. The one that faced him was nothing too special, she would make a fine convert to his cause and an excellent conquest for Harry to prove himself with. But the other woman was something else.

He could not see her face, but it was her, she was the source of the call that had dragged him from his solitude.

Lucian slowly made his way down from the elevated platform that ran around the edge of the room to the floor below. He moved between those lost in the fugue of liquor and music, their bodies pulsating to the beat of whatever DJ was in residence, and cautiously approached the table. He did not intend to make contact, but observe her from a closer perspective.

In a room filled with those on the prowl, inspired by carnal lust, it would be almost impossible to detect the eyes of the vampire lord burning deep into her soul.

As he approached a man pushed past him, causing Lucian to brush up against the woman. The moment they touched, he knew what that calling was telling him. She was his fated mate. There was no question of it, but a vampire hunter as his fated mate was as ridiculous to him as the concept had been not an hour earlier.

He stepped quickly away and disappeared into the throng before the woman could turn around. He swept around the room to where Harry and Simone were waiting.

"Invite the two women to the tower. The spa," he ordered Simone without explanation.

"That wasn't much of a hunt," Harry pouted.

"There are two women to our right that are the perfect thralls for you to bring home. I am going in search of another target," Lucian announced.

The tale of Lucian Dark has only just begun...

A reclusive vampire lord. A huntress sworn to kill him.

Fated mates cursed by their birth. Can these two hearts

heed the draw of their destiny or will it destroy them?

<u>Get Dark Tower , Book 2 in the Dark Hearts Series now!</u>